W9-CTZ-805

FOX ON STAGE

by James Marshall

PUFFIN BOOKS

For Anita Lobel

PUFFIN BOOKS
Published by the Penguin Group
Penguin Books USA Inc., 375 Hudson Street, New York, New York 10014, U.S.A.
Penguin Books Ltd, 27 Wrights Lane, London W8 5TZ, England
Penguin Books Australia Ltd, Ringwood, Victoria, Australia
Penguin Books Canada Ltd, 10 Alcorn Avenue, Toronto, Ontario, Canada M4V 3B2
Penguin Books (N.Z.) Ltd, 182–190 Wairau Road, Auckland 10, New Zealand

Penguin Books Ltd, Registered Offices: Harmondsworth, Middlesex, England

First published in the United States of America by Dial Books for Young Readers,
a division of Penguin Books USA Inc., 1993
Published in a Puffin Easy-to-Read edition, 1996

9 10

The Library of Congress has cataloged the Dial edition as follows:
Marshall, James, 1942– Fox on stage
by James Marshall.—1st edition
p. cm.
Summary: Fox makes a film for Grannie,
takes part in a magic show, and puts on a play.
ISBN 0-8037-1356-8.—ISBN 0-8037-1357-6 (lib.)
[1. Foxes—Fiction. 2. Performing arts—Fiction.] I. Title.
PZ7.M35672Fq   1993   [E]—dc20   91-46740   CIP   AC

Puffin Easy-to-Read ISBN 0-14-03.8032-9

Printed in the United States of America

Reading Level 1.9

FOX
ON FILM

When Grannie Fox had a bad spill

on the ski slopes,

she broke both legs.

"Grannie Fox will have to be

in the hospital for some time,"

said Doctor Ed.

"Old bones take longer to heal."

"Oh, what do *you* know?"

said Grannie.

But Doctor Ed was right.

Grannie had to stay in the hospital

for weeks and weeks.

"I'm so bored I could scream," she said.

"Grannie is down in the dumps," said Fox.

"We should do something to

pick up her spirits."

Then Fox got one of his great ideas.

"Louise and I are going to make
a video for Grannie," said Fox.

"How sweet," said Mom.

"But if anything happens to my camera…"

"I know what I'm doing," said Fox.

The next day the video was finished.

Fox's friends came for a look.

"This better be good," said Carmen.

"I'm very busy."

Fox put in the tape.

"Here I am taking out the trash,"
said Fox.

"This is me in my new shoes," said Fox.
"Hm," said Dexter.

"Me, flossing my teeth," said Fox.

"*How* exciting," said Carmen.

"Me again," said Fox.

"So we see," said Dexter.

11

"Care to watch it again?" said Fox.

"Certainly not," said Carmen.

"You've wasted our time."

"What was wrong with it?"
said Fox.

"It was *dumb*," said Dexter.

"I liked it, Fox," said Louise.

The next day Fox tried again.

He put a new tape in the camera
and set off.

This time he left Louise at home.

"You're so mean," said Louise.

Just down the block Fox filmed

Mrs. O'Hara trying on her new corset.

"Smile!" said Fox.

"Monster!" cried Mrs. O'Hara.

And Fox tore away.

Down a dark alley

Fox filmed some bad dogs.

They were up to no good.

"Catch that fox!" they cried.

And Fox tore away.

In the park Fox saw Officer Tom
smooching with his girlfriend.

"Nice shot!" said Fox.

"You'll be sorry!" cried Officer Tom.

But Fox got away.

Fox went to the hospital

to show Grannie his new video.

But Grannie and Louise

were already watching one.

"This is Fox flossing his teeth,"

said Louise.

"Wow!" said Grannie.

"Don't watch that!" cried Fox.

"It's dumb!"

"What do you know?" said Grannie.

"We just *love* it."

At Fox's house some folks were waiting.

"That's him!" cried Mrs. O'Hara.

Maybe they don't like being

movie stars, thought Fox.

And he went inside to face the music.

FLYING FOX

Fox and the gang

went to a magic show.

"I hope this guy is good,"

said Dexter.

"It's probably just a lot

of dumb tricks with scarves,"

said Fox.

"Anybody can do it."

And they sat down in

the very first row.

The lights went down.

And the curtain went up.

Mr. Yee, the World's Greatest Magician,
came forward.

"Welcome to the show,"
he said.

"Some parts will be *very* scary!"

"Oh, sure," whispered Fox.

"Let the magic begin!"
cried Mr. Yee.

First Mr. Yee did a trick with scarves.

"I told you," said Fox.

Then Mr. Yee made his helper vanish.

"Ho-hum," said Fox.

Next Mr. Yee pulled a rabbit from a hat.

"Big deal," said Fox.

Next Mr. Yee put his helper to sleep.

"This is *so* dumb," said Fox.

"What's all the chatter?" said Mr. Yee.

"It's Fox!" called out Dexter.

"You don't say," said Mr. Yee.

"Come up on stage, Fox."

"You're going to get it!" said Dexter.

Fox went up on stage.

"Sit here, Mr. Smarty," said Mr. Yee.

"Let's see how brave you are."

"Brave?" said Fox.

"Abracadabra!" said Mr. Yee.

Slowly the chair rose in the air.

"Where are the wires?" said Fox.

"No wires," said Mr. Yee.

"Only magic."

Fox held on tight.

And the chair flew all over.

"I'd like to come down," said Fox.

"Oh my," said Mr. Yee.

"I forgot how to do this part."

"Try Abracadabra!" said Fox.

"Abracadabra," said Mr. Yee.

Fox came gently down.

And the show was over.

At home Fox told Louise to sit down.

"Abracadabra!" said Fox.

The chair did not move.

"Rats!" said Fox.

"You just need practice," said Mom.

FOX
ON STAGE

One Saturday morning

Fox and his friends

were just lying around.

"What a sad little group,"

said Mom.

"Why don't you *do* something?"

"The television is broken,"

said Fox.

"Oh, that *is* terrible!"

said Mom.

Then Fox had one of his

great ideas.

"Let's put on a play!" he said.

"We can charge everyone a dime."

"We'll get rich!" said Dexter.

"I'll buy a new car," said Carmen.

And they went to the library.

"Let's do a spooky play," said Carmen.

"We can scare all the little kids."

"Here's what you need," said Miss Pencil.

"It's called *Spooky Plays*.

My favorite is 'The Mummy's Toe.'"

"Oooh," said the gang.

Fox and the gang went home to practice.

"The Mummy's Toe" was *very* scary.

Dexter played the mummy.

Carmen was the princess.

And Fox was the hero.

Soon things were moving right along.

Fox and Dexter worked hard

on the set.

And Carmen put up posters

all over town.

FOX
AND THE
GANG
PRESENT
"THE
MUMMY'S
TOE"

Mom and Louise helped out
with the costumes.

"Hold still," said Mom.

"I hope I'm scary enough," said Dexter.

It was time for the play.

Fox peeked out from behind the curtain.

There was a big crowd.

"I hope everything goes okay,"

said Dexter.

"What could go wrong?" said Fox.

The curtain went up.

And the play began.

Right away Carmen forgot her lines.

"Well I *did* know them,"

she said to the audience.

Then Dexter crashed through
the scenery.

"Whoops," said Dexter.

It was Fox's turn

to appear.

Suddenly it began to rain.

Fox's beautiful paper costume

fell apart in front of everyone.

"What do we do now?" said Carmen.

"Pull the curtain down!"

Fox called out to Louise.

And Louise pulled with all her might.

The curtain came down.

"Who turned out the lights?"
cried Carmen.

"Where am I?" said Dexter.

"The play is ruined!" cried Fox.

"*Everything* went wrong!"

The next day

Fox heard some folks talking.

"That Fox really knows how
to put on a funny show," someone said.
"Funniest thing I ever saw,"
said someone else.

And Fox began to plan his next show.